The Amazing Adventures of Abby McQuade
LUCKY DOLL

Evan Jacobs

Abby McQuade

Back to the Past

Daylight Saving

The Ghosts of Largo Bay

The Lady from the Caves

Lucky Doll

Mazey Pines

The Morning People

Scream Night

TV Party

Virus

EDUCATIONAL PUBLISHING
www.sdlback.com

ISBN-13: 978-1-68021-473-4
eBook: 978-1-63078-827-8

Printed in Malaysia

23 22 21 20 19   1 2 3 4 5

PACIFIC OCEAN

High School

Middle School

Abby's House

Clara's House

Mazey

Auto Shop

INDUSTIRA

SUBURBAN STATION

Train Station

Largo Bay

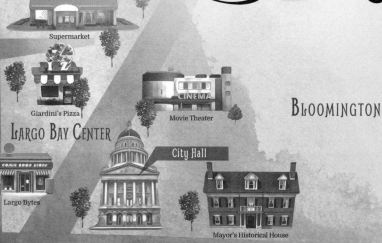

Supermarket

Giardini's Pizza

Largo Bay Center

Comic Book Store

Largo Bytes

CINEMA

Movie Theater

City Hall

Mayor's Historical House

Bloomington

Gato Villa

Adventure Begins

Trash or Treasure?

Does the furry blue doll cause bad luck? Abby and Clara throw it into the garbage.

Toy Score!

Abby discovers a rare doll. Mrs. Bernal
says she can keep it.

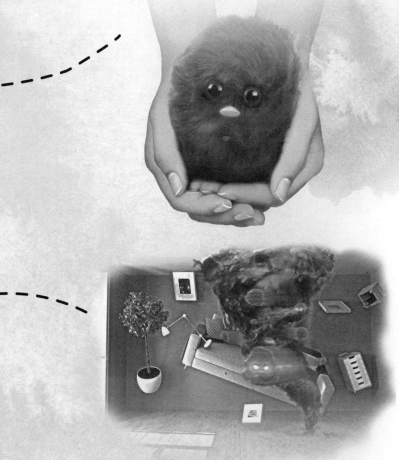

Home Invasion

Abby's house has been taken over. A tornado
of dolls swirls in her living room.

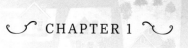

CHAPTER 1

Lucky Find

This weather is strange," Mrs. Bernal said.

Abby stood on the other side of the classroom. She looked out the window. "Huh?" she said. "I thought it was going to rain."

It had been cloudy. Now the sun was shining.

"Yeah," a student named Nikki said. She stood by the window. "It was supposed to rain."

It was now the spring semester. Largo Bay Middle School was a busy place.

Abby had chosen a new class. She was a teacher's aide. The job was in a special education classroom. Mrs. Bernal was the teacher. Some of the students were non-verbal. They didn't talk. The kids could communicate, though. They used a tablet app.

Abby loved the class. She adored the eight students. They liked her too.

Mrs. Bernal was cool. Abby respected her. Students thought she was the bomb. The teacher had a unique style. She loved animals. Her house was full of pets.

The class had a full-time aide too. Her name was Melissa. She was nice. The two women managed Abby like an adult. Students were treated with respect.

"Class, don't forget," the teacher said. "Get those permission slips signed. Or no CBI this Wednesday."

CBI meant Community Based Instruction. Mrs. Bernal took the students around the city. The town was on the small side. So it was an easy trip.

Largo Bay was on the coast. Some homes

were on the beach. Others were behind the schools. It had many strip malls. CBI trips were usually to the shops.

The students packed their backpacks. Nobody needed help. This made Abby smile.

Abby was organizing a closet. It was full of craft supplies. Then she noticed something. It was a blue furry doll. The doll was seven inches tall. It had no feet, just two black wheels. There were no arms. The eyes were black plastic. A small yellow mouth was shaped like a beak.

"Mrs. B?" She had never seen anything like it. "What is this?" she asked, holding the doll.

"Cool!" a student named Austin said. He walked over and stared at it. So did some other students.

"Oh, that old thing?" Mrs. Bernal said. "That's a Lucky doll. I bought it when I was in high school."

Abby and Austin looked at the doll. There was an on/off switch. It used batteries. What did the toy do?

"Does it work?" Abby asked.

"No," Mrs. Bernal answered. "I couldn't get it to work. It was supposed to talk."

"Really?" How exciting! A talking doll was rad.

She turned it on. Nothing happened.

"Yes," Mrs. Bernal said. The teacher sat at her desk. "It would listen to other people. Then the doll would talk. I guess mine was defective."

Abby stared at the Lucky doll. It seemed to stare back at her.

"You can have it," Mrs. Bernal said. "You seem curious about it."

"Thank you!" Abby beamed. "I'm curious by nature." She was very interested in the strange doll.

"Abby," Will Chu gasped. He held the Lucky doll. "Do you realize how rare this is?"

Will was Abby's best guy friend. He was also super smart. One day he would become a scientist. His grandfather had died of cancer. Will would cure the disease.

"These aren't made anymore. This was the first AI kids' doll. It was supposed to copy speech."

AI was artificial intelligence. The Lucky doll was teachable. It would learn as humans did.

Of course Will would know about it. He loved gadgets and computers.

"Speak English, Will!" Abby laughed. Will always talked like a scientist. "Can you get the doll to work or not?"

"How do you know it doesn't work?"

"I turned it on. Nothing happened."

"Are there batteries in it?" Will asked.

"I didn't check."

They both cracked up.

Abby turned the toy over. "We need a screwdriver."

Will looked around his bedroom. He kept it neat and tidy. There was a computer and a TV. A table was covered with phones and tablets. Next to that was his guitar and amps.

"Maybe it does work," Abby said. She took out her phone. "This doll can give my class reports."

"I doubt it," Will said. He kept searching his room. "Where is it?"

Abby checked videos online. There were some about the doll. People made shows with their dolls. The toys didn't say much.

Some videos were like unboxing demos. Kids talked about the doll's features. The doll could move on command. Pressing a button made it speak. The button was on the doll's belly. Others described the toy's history. It first came out in the late 1990s.

"Found it!" Will said, grinning.

He took out the tool. Then he flipped the doll over. Next he unscrewed the battery cover. The new batteries were in. Will closed the cover. Then he turned it on.

Abby and Will watched it. The doll seemed to stare back.

"Hello, Lucky doll," Abby said.

Nothing happened.

Then Abby remembered. She touched the button.

"Lucky!" The tone was flat. It didn't sound like today's machines.

"Move forward," Abby said.

The Lucky doll didn't move. It had a blank look.

"That's it?" Abby asked.

"For its time, it was pretty cool." Will smiled.

"Boring."

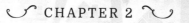

CHAPTER 2

Some Luck

"Lucky!" the doll said. Abby had just touched the doll's button.

She had played with the toy a little. It still did nothing except to say "lucky." Abby tried voice commands again. Nothing happened.

Her parents saw the doll. They didn't know anything about it. That didn't surprise their daughter. The McQuades were awesome. They were definitely not hip, though.

Abby put on her pj's. She wore gray sweats and a blue T-shirt.

Her bedroom was simple. There was her large bed. The closet was full of clothes. She had a desk too. Like most kids, she also had a

TV. It could stream shows. On the walls were photos of her friends.

Abby eyed the doll. "Maybe I should talk to you more," she said.

The doll stared blankly. Then it said, "Lucky! Lucky!"

"You need to say something else."

Then she realized she hadn't pressed the button. Abby looked at the Lucky doll.

"Lucky! Lucky!" it said again.

"Huh," she said. "You cannot talk in the middle of the night." Abby picked up the toy. She turned it off. "You're not going to ruin my beauty sleep."

Next she turned off the light. Her bed was soft and cozy. She snuggled in. *Lights off. Check. Now it's time for sleep*, she thought. *Sweet dreams to me.*

It was morning. The sun was rising. Light

streamed through the window. Abby slowly opened her eyes.

"Lucky! Lucky!"

The Lucky doll was on. This was weird. It had been turned off.

Abby got out of bed. She grabbed the doll. It stared blankly. The power switch was off.

"How are you talking?"

"Lucky! Lucky!"

Abby tried to open the battery cover. She took a small screwdriver from her desk. It wasn't the right size. "Darn it!"

Abby tried the screwdriver again. Nope. It wasn't going to work.

"Lucky! Lucky!"

"I don't have time for this. It's time for school."

"Lucky! Lucky!"

"Stop!" she ordered.

This was silly. The Lucky doll wasn't going

to stop talking. It couldn't understand her order. So she put it in her closet.

After getting ready, Abby grabbed her backpack. Then she walked into the kitchen.

The living room was next to the kitchen. A long hall ran the length of the one-story house. All rooms could be entered through it.

The front door opened into the living room. Then there were two ways to go. The family could step into the kitchen. They could walk down the hall. The hall led to the bedrooms. Abby's was first. Her parents' room was next. Another door in the hallway led to the garage.

"Morning!" Abby's mom said. She gave Abby a bowl of cereal. "I tried to time it. This mom is a cereal expert." She pointed to herself. "You don't like it soggy. I'm thinking of making a chart. Let's find your average arrival time. I can graph it too."

"Gosh, Mom," Abby said. "You are a geek. But you are the best mom. That's so nice."

Abby's mom was a loan officer. She worked in a bank. Math was her favorite subject. She played with numbers all day. It was her dream job. Abby couldn't believe it. Her mom thought math was fun!

Organic Crunchy Bites was her favorite cereal. It had cinnamon in it. Abby sat down to eat. Her mom started cleaning up.

"Is Dad here? I want to ask him about the Lucky doll. It won't stop talking."

"Is it saying more words?" her mom asked.

"Sort of." Abby ate some cereal. "It says 'lucky' on repeat."

Abby's mom laughed to herself. "Your dad had to go to work early," she said. "There was a problem."

Abby's dad owned his own business. It was a solar energy company. He was excited about it. Mr. McQuade cared about nature. The earth should be a better place for kids.

"Some solar panels detached. They fell off

a roof and into a pool. The panels are still connected to the grid. Your dad didn't want to take chances. The power was shut off on that street. Workers have to get the panels out of the pool."

Abby walked to school. She couldn't stop thinking about her dad. He was great at his job. Everyone at his work was well trained. Panels had never fallen off a roof before. It must have been bad luck.

She moved through the campus. There were three main buildings. One was for math. Another was for science. And the third was for English classrooms. There was also a small library. The office was in the front.

Students stood between the buildings. Some chatted with one another. Others were on their phones. A few read books. One or two did homework.

"Hey, Abby," Clara Erickson said. "Sorry I left before you today. I had to get here early."

The girls usually walked together. Clara had an early club meeting. Will was with her now.

Abby and Clara were best friends. They had known each other since kindergarten. The two girls dressed alike—jeans and T-shirts mostly. Sometimes they wore shorts. That was only if the weather was hot.

Clara had long brown hair. She wore it straight. It was naturally curly, though. Her skin was a nice tan color. She was a great swimmer. Every weekend there were swim meets. Clara wanted to compete in the Olympics.

"Did that doll say anything else?" Will asked.

"No," Abby sighed. "It's still saying 'lucky.' Even though I turned it off."

"What are you guys talking about?" Clara asked. She seemed unhappy.

Abby felt bad. Her friend had a crush on Will. He didn't seem to pick up on the vibe. Clara was too chicken to tell him.

She told her bestie about the Lucky doll. The bell finally rang. It was time to go to class.

The day was normal. But then Abby got to fifth period. Mrs. Bernal asked her to get some paint. It was in the craft closet. Students were going to paint portraits.

Abby opened the closet. That's when she saw it. She gasped. The Lucky doll was back!

CHAPTER 3

Lucky All Over

I thought you took it home. Maybe you forgot," Mrs. Bernal said.

"I *did* take it home," Abby said. "Do you have another one?"

"No," the teacher said. "That first one didn't work. I never bought another."

"I promise you. The Lucky doll came home with me. It was in my backpack."

Abby told her the story. Will had seen the doll. They put batteries in it. Later it wouldn't stop talking. Even off, the doll talked. Abby hadn't pressed the button either.

Then the doll said, "Lucky! Lucky!"

Had the volume gone up? Some students laughed. The doll was very rowdy.

"Can you take the batteries out?" Mrs. Bernal asked. "Its circuits are so old. They're probably fried."

"How could it still be talking?" Abby asked. She didn't expect an answer.

The teacher worked with the class.

Abby found a screwdriver. She picked up the Lucky doll. Then she left the room. No more interruptions for the students.

Outside, she sat on a planter. Abby stared at the doll. What was happening?

"Lucky! Lucky!"

The doll sounded sad. Its eyes looked different. Were they glowing? That was crazy.

Abby turned it upside down. The battery cover was stuck. She couldn't open it.

"Lucky! Lucky!"

Finally she decided to leave the toy outside. That way it wouldn't bother the class.

"The Lucky doll is here?" Will asked. He had

his backpack over one shoulder. A guitar case was in his hand.

School was over. Students were leaving. They left the campus in a steady stream.

Will and Abby walked in the other direction. They were not going with the flow. Mrs. Bernal's classroom was their target.

Abby had put the doll back in the closet. Then she went to her last two classes. Next she found Will. His last class was music.

"Tell Mrs. B we took the doll home, Will. There's no way it should be here."

"Maybe she has more than one," Will said.

"I already asked her that." Abby stopped.

Tim Cadena walked up at that moment. He carried a skateboard. "Hey, Will," he said. "Did you bring your board?"

"Not today," Will said. "I brought my guitar."

"There's no time for that." Abby frowned at Tim.

"I didn't invite you," Tim said. He smirked at her.

Tim was in eighth grade too. He was always dissing Abby. Mostly, she ignored him. Sometimes she'd clap back. The funny thing was she liked him. Maybe he liked her too.

"What's better than skateboarding?" Tim grinned. "What are you two up to?"

"I'm showing a Lucky doll to Will."

"A doll? That sounds lame to me. I don't play with dolls."

"You're lame," Abby said.

"Whatever." Tim skated away.

The two walked into Mrs. Bernal's room. The teacher was on the phone. Abby guessed she was talking to a parent. She waved at the kids.

They walked over to the closet. Abby opened it. No way! It was gone. Where was the Lucky doll?

"You should have invited me," Clara whined. "Why did you guys walk out of school together?"

Abby had left school with Will. His mom picked him up. That was when Abby bumped into Clara. Normally they walked home together. The doll had distracted her. She had forgotten.

"I went to Will's house yesterday. You were swimming. It was urgent."

The girls rounded the corner of their block. They lived across the street from each other.

"Don't use that as an excuse. You ditched me after school. Did you want to be alone with him?"

"Oh my gosh, no! I didn't. Ew!" Abby said, snorting. "I don't *like-like* him. He needed to see ..." Her voice trailed off.

Just then she heard something. It was coming from her house. The sound was clear. The girls moved closer.

"Come on!" Abby took Clara's hand. They ran toward the house.

Abby quickly unlocked the door. The girls went inside. The pair tore down the hallway. They went into Abby's bedroom.

"What's the matter?" Clara asked.

Abby stared at her desk. The Lucky doll was sitting on it. Its eyes seemed happy. Somehow the doll had moved.

"Lucky! Lucky!" it chirped.

The volume had gone up. Abby was sure of it. She looked at her closet. The door was closed. "But how did it—" Just then her phone rang.

It was Will. "Hey," he said. "Guess what? The fire department was here! It was crazy. I got home and there it was. Fire hoses were everywhere."

"The fire department?"

"Who is it?" Clara asked.

"Will," Abby told her.

Clara's face dropped. She glared at her bestie.

Abby rolled her eyes.

"My dad was working. Some chemicals exploded! His lab caught on fire!"

CHAPTER 4

Unlucky

Abby's mom was cooking dinner. "Did the fire spread? How is the rest of Will's house?" she asked.

"No," Abby said. "It didn't spread. The lab is in their garage. Some shelves burned. Will's dad says, 'safety first.' He keeps a fire extinguisher. So he put it out himself."

"Wow!" her dad said. He was making a salad. There was lettuce, tomato, and cucumber. "They got very lucky."

"Totally," Abby said. "Will's dad is super careful."

Abby looked at her parents. She loved that they cooked together. Her mom planned the menu. Her dad bought the groceries.

"Um …" She hesitated. This would sound silly. "Did it have anything to do with the Lucky doll?"

Her parents looked at her. They both laughed.

Mr. McQuade ran a hand through his short brown hair. "Abby? There's no way. That toy did not cause the fire. It was in your bedroom."

"I know the doll wasn't there. Maybe it's bad luck. It rubs off," Abby said.

"Abby?" her mom said. "I don't think—"

"Then explain the fire," Abby interrupted. "Sorry, Mom. How did Dad's solar panels fall off a roof? Everything was fine. But then I found the doll."

"It was a fluke," Abby's dad said. "The panels weren't attached right. The winds were strong yesterday. Accidents happen, honey."

"Okay," Abby said. "How did the doll get to school today? I left it here. It was in my closet.

When I came back, it was in my bedroom. But on my desk!"

"Maybe Mrs. Bernal has more than one," her dad said.

"She doesn't," Abby said.

"Well," her mom said. "She gave you the doll. Get rid of it if it's so unlucky."

This was another choice. She didn't have to keep the doll. Maybe tossing it would be for the best.

-A-

"Lucky! Lucky!" the doll said. "Lucky! Lucky!"

Abby and Clara stood by the garbage cans. The cans were in the McQuades' yard. The garage's side door was open. Outside, it was dark.

"The doll sounds scared," Clara said. "Are you sure we should toss it?"

"I don't want to," Abby said. "But it's bad luck."

Abby lifted the lid. The can was full.

"Lucky! Lucky! Lucky!" it said quickly.

"It seems to be talking faster. Is it freaked out?" Abby said.

She looked into the doll's eyes. It looked sad. How was it possible? Finally Abby put the toy into the can. It landed on some trash bags.

"Lucky! Lucky!" it cried out.

Abby dropped the lid. It landed with a *smack*. The Lucky doll kept talking. Was it a cry for help?

The girls looked at each other.

"I feel bad," Clara said.

"Me too," Abby agreed. "We'd better go inside. I don't want to change my mind."

They started to walk into the garage.

"Unlucky!" the toy said.

Abby and Clara froze. They both turned and walked to the garbage can.

Clara lifted the lid.

"Lucky! Lucky!" the doll said.

"It said 'unlucky,' Abby."

"I know."

"Lucky! Lucky!" it said again.

"This is weird," Abby said. "Let's bounce."

Clara closed the lid. "What a surprise. Not. You are a *weird* magnet."

The girls went inside. The door slammed shut behind them.

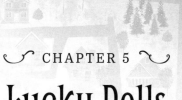

CHAPTER 5

Lucky Dolls

It was the next afternoon. Abby stood in front of her house. Dark clouds filled the sky. It was windy. Rain was coming. The garbage truck moved down the street. It was a few stops away.

The trash was at the curb. The green waste can was there too. Green waste meant leaves or grass. The city made compost. It was good for plants. There was also a can for recycling.

The truck moved in front of the house. Abby grinned. A mechanical arm came out from its side. It picked up the garbage can. Trash dropped into the back of the truck.

Relief washed over Abby. "Goodbye, Lucky,"

she whispered. There would be no more bad luck.

Suddenly the weather changed. The dark clouds parted. Rays of light broke through. Abby ignored the weird weather. It was time to have fun.

There were kids on the street. They rode bicycles. A wooden ramp had been set up. Riders launched into the air. It was rad!

Abby went over to them. She didn't notice the Lucky doll. The toy lay in the gutter. Somehow it hadn't made it into the garbage truck.

"Lucky! Lucky!" it said. It almost sounded joyful.

The sun was still shining 15 minutes later.

"I can't believe it. You want to fly off a ramp," Clara said. "That's so childish, girl. We're teenagers!"

Clara normally had swim practice. Her coach had given the team the day off. They had placed first at a big meet. It had been in Bloomington.

Bloomington was nearby. Abby and Clara thought the town was weird. The people seemed odd. They didn't go there much.

Clara sat on her bike. Abby was next to her. She was on her bike too. A black helmet rested low on her head.

The wooden ramp was 50 yards away.

"It's going to be epic!" Abby cried. "Watch me get air."

Both girls laughed.

A small crowd had formed around them. Kids wanted to see Abby fly.

Abby took off. She pedaled faster and faster. The ramp was just ahead.

The sky got cloudy. More clouds blocked the sun. It got darker again.

Abby didn't notice. She kept pedaling hard. Her bike touched the ramp. The wheel didn't go up. Instead, the ramp began to crumble.

She hit the brakes. The cruiser started to skid.

"Aaahhh!" she cried.

The bike went down. It had broken the ramp! Abby wiped out. In the tumble, she skinned her leg.

Clara and the other kids ran over. "Are you okay?" Clara asked.

"Yeah," Abby groaned. "Ouch!" She lay on her back. Pain shot up her side. "How bad does my leg look?"

"Your jeans aren't torn. I can't see through them." Clara picked up Abby's bike. She moved it out of the way. Some kids helped her to stand.

"You were going so fast!" a kid said. "It looked like you were going to fly away!"

"Maybe next time," Abby said. "See you guys later." She limped over to her bike.

The girls walked their bikes toward Abby's house.

"I can't believe I broke the ramp. The Lucky doll is gone," Abby said. "My luck should have changed. What's up?"

"Remember the maple stick problem?" Clara asked.

"What? I don't get the connection. The pain has affected my brain," Abby said.

"The sticks gave kids a rash. Remember the bugs? They brought bad luck."

"Those bugs wanted to rule the world. How is it the same?"

"Maybe the doll wants to rule."

"Hmm, interesting idea," Abby said.

The pair got closer to home. Abby heard something. It was a familiar sound.

"Lucky! Lucky! Lucky!"

It was the Lucky doll. And it was talking fast.

Abby dropped her bike onto the grass. Clara did the same. They burst into the house. The girls ran into Abby's room.

What? There were two Lucky dolls! The dolls were on Abby's desk.

"Lucky! Lucky! Lucky!" both dolls said.

The girls heard rustling. It came from the closet. Abby went over and opened it.

Two more dolls were inside! Abby grabbed them. She turned them over.

"What are you doing?" Clara asked.

"I'm looking for the on switch."

"Are they on?"

"No!" Abby said.

"Only you, Abby." Clara shook her head. "This is like the movie *Gremlins*."

"At least Gizmo was sweet. Nobody warned us about the doll. The boy in the movie didn't follow the rules. We don't even *know* the rules."

Abby suddenly knew what to do.

CHAPTER 6

Gordon Looper

The Lucky doll?" Amtrak Eddie cackled.

He ran his hand through his bushy black hair. Amtrak Eddie was Abby's favorite uncle. To him, Abby's adventures were great. His advice was always on point.

Eddie was an Amtrak train engineer. He had been one for 20 years. There were crazy things in the world. Some were normal. Others were supernatural. Eddie had seen both.

"You know about the doll?" Abby asked.

"Oh yeah."

Abby looked at Clara. They were both eating chocolate donuts. Clara's had rainbow sprinkles. Abby's was covered in powdered sugar. Eddie drank coffee.

The girls had met him at the train station. They rode their bikes there.

Abby knew her uncle's schedule. They met up whenever they could. Sometimes it was just to talk about life.

"I moved a shipment of Lucky dolls once," Eddie said.

The station had a small food court. There were outside tables. The tables were near the tracks. Eddie stared at them.

"Gosh, that was a long time ago. Maybe 20 years have passed."

"That's when the doll came out," Abby said. "Did you ever own one? Do they bring bad luck?"

"Or multiply on their own?" Clara asked.

"Hmm …" Amtrak Eddie's eyes narrowed. "I've never owned one. Beats me."

They told him everything that had

happened. Eddie looked into the distance. Was he even listening? Abby's uncle seemed to be lost in thought.

"That's right!" He snapped his fingers. "Got it! I had to deal with the creator directly. He was a real pill. His name was Gordon Looper."

"Gordon Looper?" Abby said.

Clara tried not to laugh.

"Yes, that was his name." Eddie looked at his niece. "Gordon Looper. He didn't trust how workers handled the dolls. No forklifts allowed. Back then the Lucky doll was selling well. That made him happy. Big companies were jealous. They ruined his marketing."

"Other companies tried to put him out of business?" Abby asked.

"That's what Looper thought," Eddie said. "Was it true? Who knows? He claimed to be a master inventor. But none of his other dolls had sold. Big companies were squeezing him out, he said. The man bragged about sales.

The doll was the most successful product he had ever made. Big toy makers wanted his patent. No way would he ever sell it. This made competitors angry."

"Why didn't he sell?" Clara asked. "He could've made even more money. If he was a master, then invent another doll."

"The man was an artist," Abby said. "The Lucky doll was probably like his child. Am I right?"

"That's exactly what he thought." Eddie took a sip of coffee. "You never forget a man like Looper. His factory caught fire. It ruined him. That ended his business. The factory was in Flowerville. It's a really small town. Maybe 100 people live there. He told me he would never move."

Abby took out her phone. She did a quick search on Gordon Looper. "Here's an address," she said. "I wonder if he still lives there."

"Isn't Flowerville, like, three hours away?" Clara asked. "How are we going to get there? We can't ride our bikes. Maybe we should call him."

"There's no number listed," Abby said.

"Your next adventure found you," Amtrak Eddie said.

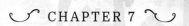

CHAPTER 7

Flowerville

I don't know how you do it," Aunt Jackie said.

"That's not true!" Abby cried.

Aunt Jackie was driving. Abby was in the passenger seat. Clara was in the back. Both girls held their phones.

It had been raining for 10 minutes. Then it stopped. The sun came out.

"It is true!" Aunt Jackie said. She eyed the rearview mirror. Her hand brushed hair off her face. "I tell myself, 'Jackie, she's a teen.' But this trip and drive? It's a lot to ask, girls!"

"I know," Abby said with a sigh. "You are the best aunt ever." She patted Jackie's shoulder. "Clara and I totally appreciate it."

"I'm with you, Aunt Jackie," Clara said. "I'm over these adventures too."

Jackie was Abby's mom's sister. She was a legal researcher. Facts were always at her fingertips. Her curiosity for learning matched Abby's. She was close to her niece. This was a big reason why.

Abby's aunt always had relationship drama. She usually talked about her failed first dates. The girls loved her determination. She kept trying to find her soul mate.

"This will be a quick visit," Abby said. "I just want to see if Mr. Looper will help us. You can wait in the car. It's fine with me, Aunt Jackie."

"Can I wait in the car too?" Clara asked. She was looking at her phone.

"Uh, no," Abby said. "You're just mad about Will. I'm not into him. But Tim? Maybe I have a little crush. When he's not being lame."

"Ha! You think I'm driving three hours for nothing? No way am I sitting in the car. This man could be a total creep. I'll go with you," Jackie said. "But you do all the talking."

Gordon Looper lived in a tiny red house. There was a large field behind it. It was full of dirt. The home was on a corner. No other houses were nearby.

"So much for Flowerville. This place looks weird," Aunt Jackie said. "We're staying in the car till I get more info."

Jackie took out her tablet. She started to search for information. Her job gave her access to powerful websites. Abby's aunt could find out anything about anyone.

"His house is cute," Abby said. "It kind of looks like mine."

The grass was dead in the front yard. There was a bench near the porch. Some dolls sat on it. A few were missing arms. Others were missing heads. A life-sized doll stood by the front door. It wore a suit.

"Yeah, sure," Clara said. "If you had a bunch of junky dolls around. Oh, let's not forget the dead grass."

"Well," Aunt Jackie said. "After the Lucky doll, he never made others. He got a job at a fast-food chain. The man has worked there ever since."

"How sad," Abby sighed. "He just gave up. Maybe he'll help us."

Abby got out of the car. Aunt Jackie and Clara followed. They waited for a car to pass. Then they crossed the street.

"If Looper gets weird, we're out," Aunt Jackie stated. "No going inside! Not even if he insists."

"Okay," Abby said.

"I'm in total agreement," said Clara.

They moved across the dead grass. Doll parts covered the ground. There were heads, arms, and bodies.

"This is gross. It looks like a serial killer lives here," Clara said.

"Shhh!" Abby and Aunt Jackie shushed.

They moved closer to the front door. Suddenly it opened. Gordon Looper stepped out. He slammed the door behind him.

Looper was short and pudgy. His hair was brown and bushy. He wore his work uniform. It was a little tight.

"All right," the man said. "I've told you kids a million times. No Girl Scout cookies!"

"We're not selling cookies. My name is Abby McQuade. I'm from Largo Bay. This is my aunt Jackie and my best friend, Clara."

"Nice to meet you," Gordon said. He locked the door. "Now go!"

Looper started to walk past them.

"But, sir," Abby said. "We have some questions."

"I don't have time for chitchat," the man barked. "I'm going to be late for work. Being the manager comes with responsibilities."

"We're here about the Lucky doll."

Looper stopped. He looked at Abby. "There's nothing to say," he said. "I don't make dolls anymore. The toy business is dead to me."

"But why?" Abby asked.

"Why indeed?" Looper moved closer. "Because I've never been successful!"

The man pointed to the dolls on the bench. He waved to the doll parts scattered around.

"Then I made the Lucky doll. They took it from me. All the big toy companies wanted it. Everyone wanted my patent. They knew I was a genius. But I wouldn't sell it! I'll never sell it."

"Why not?" Clara asked.

"Because it's mine! All mine. They couldn't

take it. The competition knew I had one factory. The Lucky doll would be bad for their business. So they burned my factory to the ground!"

"That's a serious charge. You don't know that," Aunt Jackie said. "It was a factory. Accidents happen all the time. Maybe a wire sparked."

"That's right," Abby said. "Fires happen everywhere. It could have just been a coincidence."

"Well, it wasn't!" Looper said. He frowned. The man was filled with rage. "But I had the last laugh. Even with the fire, I filled every order. Then I stopped making the doll. But there was a special doll. It was the last one I ever made." He laughed wildly. "I paid a witch. She cast a spell. It was black magic. The doll would spread bad luck. It would also duplicate itself to infinity."

"Why would you do that?" Abby asked.

She was starting to get mad. "Especially since they bought *your* doll?"

"Because I've had nothing but bad luck!" Looper shrieked. "Everyone should know how it feels."

Something clicked for Abby. It all made sense now.

Mrs. Bernal had bought the last Lucky doll. It never worked. That was its way of giving her bad luck. The teacher had been "lucky." It could have been worse.

Then Abby found it. She had put in new batteries. The doll got energized. Now it was spreading bad luck. It was multiplying too! The curse was real.

"I will not help you," Looper said. He barged past them. "I made the darn doll. Big companies tried to ruin me. All I've had is bad luck. Nobody cares. Now it is someone else's turn."

Abby, Clara, and Jackie watched him walk away.

"What, no car?" Clara asked.

"Want a ride to work?" Abby called out.

"No!" the man yelled. "I don't want anything from you! Leave me alone!"

"Fine!" Abby cried. "I wanted the doll to work. It was for the kids in my classroom. Who doesn't want to make kids smile and laugh? Especially those with special needs. Apparently you! That was the only reason. Otherwise, I would have left your crazy doll alone!"

Looper kept walking.

"I think we should go," Jackie said firmly.

CHAPTER 8

Too Many Dolls

I need some water," Clara said. They walked up to Abby's house. "It's too hot outside."

The sky was overcast when they left. Now the sun was out. It beat down on them. The air felt thick.

"I feel bad for Mr. Looper," Abby said. She put her key into the lock.

"Why?" Clara asked. "You tried to be nice to him. He was so rude to us."

"Wouldn't you be? He feels like something was taken from him."

"He is bitter. I wouldn't be like that. It eats up your insides."

"Good point."

Abby pushed the front door open.

Something blue flew at their heads. The pair ducked. The blue object smashed into the wall. Then it landed on the floor. Blank eyes stared at them.

It was a Lucky doll!

"What in the world?" Abby cried.

The girls looked around the living room. Lucky dolls swirled around. They were flying! More dolls came from Abby's room.

The swarm of dolls got bigger. They were growing in number.

"Abby," Clara yelled. "What is going on?"

"The Lucky dolls are multiplying! Mr. Looper's bad luck will spread."

The dolls slammed into a bookcase. A TV was knocked off the wall. It landed with a thud. The crazy blue toys flew into paintings. They broke glass knickknacks.

Abby grabbed Clara. They moved into the kitchen. Oh no! There were even more Lucky dolls there!

The dolls rammed the stove. They dented the refrigerator. One doll switched on the oven. Another slammed into a window.

"Don't let them escape!" Abby called. "It will unleash bad luck! Mr. Looper used black magic."

"Let's get out of here!" Clara cried.

The girls ducked.

Lucky dolls flew into the wall.

Boom! Boom! Boom!

They dropped to the floor.

Even more dolls came from Abby's room. Soon the girls were trapped. They were covered in a tornado of dolls.

The Lucky dolls hit their legs. They smacked the girls' arms and backs. There was no escape.

"My room is too far!" Abby yelled. "Let's leave through the garage. But how? We can't move. Too many dolls are in the way."

"Let's at least try," Clara begged.

Abby and Clara tried to move. They were trapped in the storm of blue. Dolls were still coming at them.

The living room was filling up. Toys were three feet deep. Pretty soon the house would be full.

The sliding door was near. It led to the backyard. The door was only a few feet away. There was a problem, though. Too many Lucky dolls blocked the way.

More and more dolls appeared. They would keep multiplying. The house would explode them. Then they would spill out into the street. The dolls would fly away. Looper's bad luck would be everywhere.

"Abby?" Clara called. "Think! What should we do?"

The Lucky dolls kept coming. They covered the windows. The house got dark. The girls had trouble seeing.

Soon all the light would be blocked.

Abby forced her arm through the toys. She felt the door handle. Where was the lock? If only she could flip it.

The swirl of dolls slowed. Abby's living room was stacked from floor to ceiling.

There it was! She'd found the lock.

Just then a ray of light broke through. It parted the sea of blue.

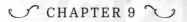

CHAPTER 9

Giant Lucky

The front door had opened. How? Abby didn't care. More light poured into the living room.

For a second the swirling stopped. There stood Gordon Looper. He was in his work uniform.

The dolls in the living room were stacked high. The girls could barely see him.

"All right!" Gordon yelled. "Enough of this bad luck! I created you, Lucky dolls. The evil spell was my fault. I command you to halt."

The swirling stopped. None of the dolls moved. Their eyes glowed.

Abby and Clara looked at each other. They couldn't move. There were too many Lucky dolls.

"Well," Mr. Looper said smugly. "Let's start cleaning up. Is everyone ready?"

"Lucky!" a doll said.

"Lucky!" another called.

Soon the toys were chanting.

"Lucky! Lucky!"

The chorus grew louder. The racket was deafening.

"Lucky! Lucky! Lucky!"

Abby and Clara covered their ears. They looked at Mr. Looper. He covered his ears too! "Stop it!" he yelled. "No more! It's over!"

The Lucky dolls started to sway. Their movement was slow and steady. Then they started bumping into one another.

"Lucky! Lucky!" they chanted.

Something was different. The girls were worried.

The dolls moved as one. They met in the center of the living room. Suddenly there was one giant Lucky doll. The dolls had transformed!

It was five feet tall. Two huge eyes stared blankly. The blue was almost blinding. A yellow plastic beak opened and shut. Chomp! Chomp! Two large tires that were its feet marked up the floor.

Its eyes glowed. They stared right at Gordon Looper!

"Mr. Looper!" Abby called. She grabbed him.

With a yank, Abby opened the sliding door. The three humans ran into the backyard. The giant Lucky doll followed them outside.

Abby ran to the side gate. Clara followed her. Mr. Looper was behind them.

The iron gate opened. Abby, Clara, and Mr. Looper ran into the street.

The giant toy came after them. It sounded like a jet engine.

Vroom! Vroom!

"Aaahhh!" the three screamed. The street was deserted. Nobody came to help.

The Lucky doll's eyes narrowed. What was it up to? There was a grin on its face.

The three people turned down another street.

Bam! Bam!

The doll smashed into some garbage cans. Then it tore through some bushes. Giant Lucky smashed flowers in its path. Anything in its way was crushed.

Gordon started to wheeze. He breathed heavily.

"Are you okay?" Abby asked.

"I have asthma," he gasped. "There's no way I can keep up. You two had better let me go. The Lucky doll is mad at me. I deserve it. This is all my fault anyway."

They were near a small park. It was close to the middle school. There were swings. The playground also had a climbing frame and slides. Families liked to picnic there.

"There's a bench in the park," Abby said. "You can rest there."

"But what about my Lucky doll? It will get us for sure!"

"Don't worry!" Abby said.

"Did you see that doll?" Clara hissed. "All I can do is worry!"

Abby grabbed Mr. Looper's arm. She motioned to her bestie. The three ran into the park.

The Lucky doll followed. It tore up the lawn as it went. Clods of dirt and grass flew everywhere.

There was nowhere else to run. Abby looked around. Two brick walls blocked the other side of the park. It was supposed to keep kids safe. Not now! The three were trapped.

Mr. Looper collapsed onto a bench. He huffed and puffed. The girls sat next to him.

"Thank you, girls," he said. "Now go. This is my toy. I'll deal with it."

"We're not leaving you," Abby said.

The giant doll slowly rolled up to them. There was nowhere to go. Nobody could escape now.

"Um, Abby?" Clara said. "What are we going to do?"

"I don't know," Abby said slowly.

"Great ..." Clara's voice trailed off.

The girls stood. They blocked Mr. Looper from the doll.

Abby suddenly felt mad. "You're supposed to be lucky!" she yelled.

Giant Lucky inched closer. It snapped its large beak.

"You are not helping," Clara said. "Abby, chill out."

The doll moved closer. It was inches from the girls. Again, it snapped its beak.

Abby took Clara's hand. "We're not afraid!" she said defiantly.

The giant started to open its beak again.

Dark clouds blocked the sun. Then the sky seemed to open. The rain came down in sheets. In seconds the humans were soaked.

Zap! Zap!

The Lucky doll made a noise. Sparks shot out of it. Then the giant toy started to spin on its wheels. Faster and faster it went.

Zap!

The doll stopped moving.

The girls could see smoke. Giant Lucky started to shrink. It got smaller.

Eventually the giant was no more. The doll was back to its normal size. It was Mrs. Bernal's doll again. The glow in its eyes was gone.

CHAPTER 10

Still Lucky?

The rain slowly stopped. Now it was just a light drizzle. The sprinkles felt nice. A hot situation was suddenly cool.

"Sorry about your toy," Abby said.

"No, don't be sorry," Mr. Looper said. He picked up the lone Lucky doll. "It was all me. I should apologize."

"Why did you help us?" Clara asked.

"Oh, good question." Abby nodded at Clara. Then she looked at Mr. Looper. "You were so rude before."

"I know." The man sighed. He stared at them. "I'm sorry about that too. I didn't want to help. But then you said something. You wanted the doll to work for those kids.

It touched my heart. Do you want to know why?"

The girls stared at him. He was tearing up.

"I have a son. His name is Lucky. The doll was named after him. Lucky has autism. Those dolls were my gift to him."

Abby looked at Clara. "Autism is a developmental disorder. It makes it hard for some people to communicate. There are challenges with social skills. Each person is unique, just like we are."

Clara nodded. She'd never worked with Mrs. Bernal's students.

"How did you know where to find me?" Abby asked.

"GPS." Gordon held up the Lucky doll. "I put a system into each doll. They could be tracked. I didn't want kids to lose them. Back then, cell phones were new. Nobody could guess how popular they would become. But I knew."

It stopped drizzling. The sun came out.

Mr. Looper didn't seem to notice. "Tracking was a new feature. People could use their phones to find their dolls. But then I went out of business."

"Maybe your luck is changing," Abby said.

"It has started to change," the man said. "A company asked me to create an app. I didn't want to. But my son uses a tablet. So I said yes. It just got released."

"Whoa, that's cool," Clara said. "Maybe now you can make new toys."

Mr. Looper smiled. It was the first time the girls had seen him smile. "I had better get going," he said. "Flowerville is far away. Thank you, girls. You helped me to see what's important. Maybe it's time to start inventing again."

"Oh, that sounds rad," Abby said. "Can you leave the black magic out this time?"

"Yes, for sure," Gordon said, laughing.

With that, he walked away. They watched him go.

"See, Clara?" Abby said. "Aren't you glad we went to his house?"

"Yeah, I guess."

The pair started to walk back to Abby's.

"Maybe we can stay in touch with Mr. Looper."

"Why?" Clara asked.

"I don't know. He seems like he needs us. We're nice to him. Maybe he'll name a doll *Abby*."

"No. I like the name *Clara* better."

Abby laughed. "Whatever."

"I doubt he'll create an Abby doll," Clara said.

The girls lived on the next street. They turned toward their block.

"Lucky! Lucky!"

Abby's eyes got wide. She looked at her bestie. Clara had turned pale.

"Did you just hear—" Abby started.

"Lucky! Lucky!"

"Abby!" Clara said. "The Lucky doll is still here! But Mr. Looper is gone."

They heard another sound. Skateboards were coming their way.

The girls turned. Will and Tim skated toward them. Tim was holding his phone.

"Hey, Abby." Tim smiled. "I like Lucky dolls now." He held up his phone. A red Lucky doll was on the screen. Tim tapped it.

"Lucky! Lucky!" it said.

"Double tap," Will said. "The doll gets louder."

"You said Lucky dolls were lame." Abby grinned at him.

"So lame," Tim said. "But this isn't a Lucky doll. It's the Lucky doll *app*. Apps are cool."

"Uh-huh," Abby said with a shrug.

"Call me lucky," Clara said. "But only if I never hear the word *lucky* again."

Abby laughed.

"What are you guys doing?" Will asked. "Come skating with us."

Abby stood next to Tim. Will and Clara were standing close together. Everything was back to normal. If teenagers were normal, Abby thought.

Clara nodded. She really wanted to hang out with the boys.

"Sure," Abby said. "We'll get our bikes."

"Cool," Tim said. He tapped his phone.

"Lucky! Lucky!" the app said.

The girls made a face.

"Um, Tim?" Abby said. "Could you stop it?"

"Okay," he agreed.

Abby and Clara went to get their bikes.

"Lucky! Lucky!"

Abby turned. She looked at Tim. "Dude!" she said. "Stop it!"

"He just deleted it." Will laughed.

"Okay," Abby said. She walked toward her house.

Abby thought she heard the doll again. This time she wasn't sure. The words were stuck in her head. How many times had she heard them?

"Lucky! Lucky!"

Abby shook it off. Perhaps the toy was still talking. Was there another doll nearby? Maybe.

This town was full of surprises. It was the perfect home for Abby McQuade.

The Amazing Adventures of
Abby McQuade

More Amazing Adventures with Abby

BACK TO THE PAST
978-1-68021-470-3

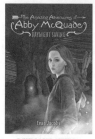

DAYLIGHT SAVING
978-1-68021-474-1

THE GHOSTS OF LARGO BAY
978-1-68021-466-6

THE LADY FROM THE CAVES
978-1-68021-471-0

LUCKY DOLL
978-1-68021-473-4

MAZEY PINES
978-1-68021-469-7

THE MORNING PEOPLE
978-1-68021-472-7

SCREAM NIGHT
978-1-68021-468-0

VIRUS
978-1-68021-467-3